There's Only One You!

There's Only One You!

By Dean Walley

Illustrated by Vivian Taylor

♛ Hallmark Children's Editions

THERE'S ONLY ONE YOU!

Christmas 1970

Dear Mary Ann —

with love,

Carol

You see so many different kinds of people —
in the park — on the street where you live —
in the store where mommy takes you shopping.

Do any of these people look like you? No!
There's only one you. You're special!

If you're a boy, people may say you look a little bit like your father.

If you're a girl, people may say you look
a little bit like your mother.
But, most of all, you
look like you!

Take a look in the mirror and you'll see
some of the things that make you you.

You have a special kind of nose. Your
eyes are special, too. And no one else
can smile a smile exactly as you do.

The way you look isn't the only thing
that makes you you.

You see a lot of pretty things
that other people miss. That's why
they're surprised sometimes when you say,
"Look at this!" And they're glad you told them.

If you listen, you can hear things that no one else can hear. Like marbles rolling across the floor, and breezes puffing at the door, and kittens saying "I want more!" Little sounds that only your little ears can hear.

Nobody talks like you either.
You use the same words that
everybody uses, but you put
them together in a special way.
You say funny things and smart
things, too. That's why your
mother and father are always
telling people things that you say.

The way you feel is another reason that there's only one you.

Sometimes you feel giggily—sometimes wiggily.

Sometimes you're glad
and sometimes
you're sad — or mad!

How do you feel
right now? Are you
feeling happy that
there's only one you?

No one else does the
nice things you do.

And that makes people
do nice things for you.

Your friends think you're a special person—that's why they like to be with you.

Your parents *know* there's only one you,
and that's why they love you so much.

Aren't you glad that there's nobody

quite like you in the whole, wide world?

Isn't it nice to be you?